UNICORN ACADEMY

NATURE MAGIC

Shimmer smacked his hoof to the floor with a *bang*. A tiny bolt of magic shot from his hoof, crisscrossing over the grass and hitting a stone. *CRACK!* The stone shattered, leaving a strong, sugary smell hanging in the air.

★ ★ ★

LOOK OUT FOR MORE
ADVENTURES WITH

UNICORN ACADEMY
NATURE MAGIC

Lily *and* Feather
Phoebe *and* Shimmer
Zara *and* Moonbeam
Aisha *and* Silver

UNICORN ACADEMY

NATURE MAGIC 2

Phoebe and Shimmer

JULIE SYKES
illustrated by LUCY TRUMAN

A STEPPING STONE BOOK™
Random House New York

Text copyright © 2020 by Julie Sykes and Linda Chapman
Cover art and interior illustrations copyright © 2020 by Lucy Truman

All rights reserved. Published in the United States by Random House Children's Books, a division of Penguin Random House LLC, New York. Originally published in paperback in the United Kingdom by Nosy Crow Ltd, London, in 2020.

Random House and the colophon are registered trademarks and A Stepping Stone Book and the colophon are trademarks of Penguin Random House LLC.

Visit us on the Web! rhcbooks.com

Educators and librarians, for a variety of teaching tools, visit us at RHTeachersLibrarians.com

Library of Congress Cataloging-in-Publication Data
Names: Sykes, Julie, author. | Truman, Lucy, illustrator.
Title: Phoebe and Shimmer / Julie Sykes ; illustrated by Lucy Truman.
Description: First American edition. | New York : Random House Children's Books, [2021] | Series: Unicorn Academy Nature Magic ; 2 | "A Stepping Stone book." | Audience: Ages 6-9. | Summary: When a freak weather event puts everyone in danger during a Unicorn Academy trip to the coast, Shimmer's newfound magic might be able to save them, if they can think fast and be very brave.
Identifiers: LCCN 2020050449 (print) | LCCN 2020050450 (ebook) | ISBN 978-0-593-42672-2 (paperback) | ISBN 978-0-593-42673-9 (lib. bdg.) | ISBN 978-0-593-42674-6 (ebook)
Subjects: CYAC: Unicorns—Fiction. | Magic—Fiction. | Friendship—Fiction. | Boarding schools—Fiction. | Schools—Fiction.
Classification: LCC PZ7.S98325 Pho 2021 (print) | LCC PZ7.S98325 (ebook) | DDC [E]—dc23

Printed in the United States of America
10 9 8 7 6 5 4 3 2 1
First American Edition

For Hettie and Maddie, who love magic.
May you always believe in fairies
and unicorns.

CHAPTER 1

"You'll never guess what I just saw!" Phoebe exclaimed, bursting into Amethyst dorm. Her eyes sparkled with excitement. "Well?" she said, looking around eagerly at her dorm mates—Zara, Lily, and Aisha. "Come on, guess!"

"No time. You can tell us later," said Zara, pulling her hoodie over her dark brown hair.

"Yes, hurry up now, Phoebe, or we'll be late for the cross-country ride with Ms. Tulip," said Lily. Aisha didn't say anything. She was too busy looking for something under her bed.

"But this is important!" Phoebe said. She wanted

her friends to feel the same excitement she did. "Okay, so this is what happened," she said, going into what Zara called her storytelling mode. "I was coming back from breakfast, just walking in the hall, minding my own business, when I saw Ms. Rosemary and Ms. Rivers whispering together outside Ms. Nettles's office. They left, and I heard Ms. Nettles making a weird noise, so I sneaked a look around the door, and guess what?" Phoebe paused dramatically as she remembered what she had seen in the headteacher's office. "Ms. Nettles was really upset!"

Her friends continued to get ready, not looking up.

"She was crying!" Phoebe said, to get their attention. "Loudly, with lots of tears. Well, what do you think about that?"

"Found it!" Aisha crawled out from under her bed. She was clutching a purple hoodie. "Who was sighing?"

"Ms. Nettles was *crying*," said Phoebe, looking around at her friends. "Don't you think that is super weird? Headteachers don't cry. Something must be going on!"

"Was Ms. Nettles really crying, Phoebe?" Zara said, raising her eyebrows. "Or are you just exaggerating like usual?"

"No! I'm not!" Phoebe insisted. "I promise, Ms. Nettles was a hundred percent crying. She blew her nose and it sounded as loud as an elephant trumpeting!"

"Oh, I hope she's okay," said Lily, looking concerned.

Zara frowned. "I'm sure she is. There's probably a simple reason. She could have been tearing up because her allergies came back."

Phoebe rolled her eyes. "You are *so* boring, Zara!"

"Not boring, just logical," said Zara with a grin. "Seriously, there's been enough drama happening here without having to make stuff up, Phoebe. Purple tornadoes sweeping across the island, the school almost being destroyed, a strange voice in the tornado saying they're not going to be stopped . . ."

"Aha! But maybe those things have something to do with Ms. Nettles's crying," said Phoebe. "Maybe something else has happened and she's found out about it! Maybe there's been another tornado or something even"—she paused dramatically—"*worse!*"

"Or maybe Ms. Nettles just has allergies," said

Zara again. "It is springtime after all, and there's a lot of pollen in the air."

Lily turned to Phoebe. "Come on, Phoebe. We really have to go. We'll be in trouble with Ms. Tulip if we're late."

Phoebe sighed. She brushed her long honey-blond hair before braiding it. She loved her three friends in Amethyst dorm, but she sometimes felt they really didn't get her. She liked to make everything seem as exciting as possible, but they seemed to just want to know the facts. How boring was that?

Shimmer will want to hear about Ms. Nettles, she told herself as she got ready. A warm glow spread through her as she thought of her handsome unicorn. Shimmer loved drama and storytelling just as much as she did. *He's the best,* Phoebe thought happily as she followed the others to the stables. *I'm so glad Ms. Nettles paired me with him.*

She'd never forget that first day at Unicorn Academy—arriving at the school and seeing the beautiful glass-and-marble building glittering in the sunlight, meeting the rest of her dorm, and being paired with her own perfect unicorn. Students arrived at the academy in January when they were ten and stayed a whole year. During that time, they got to know their unicorn and learned all about Unicorn Island. Once they were older, they could become guardians of the island.

"Look at all the flowers," said Lily as they made their way across the lawn. She pointed to the beds of bright spring bulbs—tulips, bluebells, and daffodils waving their yellow heads in the morning breeze. "Aren't they beautiful?"

Phoebe stooped to pick a daffodil, thinking that it would look nice in her hair. She froze as she heard an angry shout.

"Stop right there!" It was Ms. Bramble, the head gardener. She stomped over with a rake in her hand. "I hope you weren't about to pick a daffodil."

"Definitely not. I would never do that, Ms. Bramble." Phoebe shook her head hard and tried to look as innocent as possible. "Flowers should be left in the ground for everyone to enjoy. I was just bending over to . . . to smell them."

Ms. Bramble didn't look like she believed her. "Hmm. Very well. Hurry along, then. You're crushing the grass!"

"Yes, Ms. Bramble," said Phoebe politely, wondering why the gardener was so grumpy. People often picked the daffodils. There were hundreds of them.

As she ran after her friends, she mimicked Ms. Bramble's expression: first mad, then suspicious. Phoebe loved watching people so that

she could copy them later. Her old drama teacher had taught her that, to make acting come alive, you had to draw on real-life experiences. "Hurry along now, girls! You're crushing the grass!" she said, wagging her finger at her friends and mimicking Ms. Bramble's voice.

They giggled and continued on to the stables.

Shimmer whinnied when he saw Phoebe. He was a tall unicorn with a long pink-and-pale-blue mane that fell over his deep brown eyes. His thick tail flowed to the ground like a waterfall. "Are you looking forward to going around the cross-country course, Phoebe?" he asked. "Is it a race this time? I bet we could win a race! I can jump really high, and I'm faster than all the other unicorns!"

"I know you are," said Phoebe proudly. She brushed Shimmer's coat, then carefully combed out the tangles in his mane and tail. As she worked, she told him about the teachers and their strange behavior.

"*No!* Really?" he exclaimed, opening his eyes wide. "Ms. Bramble *yelled* at you, and you saw Ms. Nettles *crying* at her desk! That's terrible. I'll ask the other unicorns if they know anything about it."

"Yes, please do that!" said Phoebe, happy that

at least Shimmer believed her news. "The others think I'm exaggerating, but I'm absolutely *sure* something is going on."

They went out into the yard, where there was a noisy group of students and unicorns. Amethyst dorm shared riding lessons with the students from Opal and Topaz dorms. Ms. Tulip was late arriving. She was small and energetic, and her lessons were always a lot of fun, but today she seemed distracted.

"It's bad news, I'm afraid," she said, clapping her hands for quiet. "The cross-country ride is canceled. Ms. Nettles has asked that we clean the stables and yard instead. Everything has to look as neat and shiny as a new hoof pick. I'm sorry," she added, raising her hands to silence the groans.

"Can't we just do a few jumps? You know we'll

work harder if we can do some jumping first," Spike from Topaz dorm said, leading a chorus of "Come on, Ms. Tulip. Please say yes!"

Ms. Tulip shook her head. "Unicorn Academy is being inspected. But if there's enough time, you can go for a quick ride once you're done cleaning."

Phoebe gasped. "Are they thinking of closing the school?"

"Of course not, Phoebe," said Ms. Tulip. "It's just an inspection. But naturally Ms. Nettles and all of the staff want to show the academy at its best and highlight all the wonderful things we do here. So let's get started. Topaz dorm, you can clean the yard; Opal, the storeroom; and Amethyst, the big barn next door. When you've finished, you can head out for a ride in your dorm groups. But remember not to jump without me!"

Phoebe lowered her voice. "I absolutely bet this inspection was the reason Ms. Nettles was crying earlier!" she hissed to Zara, Lily, and Aisha. Their unicorns went sadly back to their stables to wait for them, and they walked to the barn to start cleaning up. "Do you think she's in trouble because she and the teachers left us here alone when that purple tornado almost hit the school?"

"Possibly," said Zara thoughtfully. "It was really dangerous."

"The school could have been destroyed if Feather hadn't discovered her moving magic in time and diverted the tornado out to the ocean," said Aisha. She smiled at Lily. "You and Feather were amazing. Her magic is awesome."

Lily blushed. "Thanks." Feather was the only Amethyst dorm unicorn who had discovered their magic. Each young unicorn at the academy had a

special power. Some, like Feather, discovered theirs quickly, while others took longer. Those unicorns who hadn't found their magic and bonded with their partner by the end of the year had to stay at Unicorn Academy for a second year.

Phoebe hoped that Shimmer would find his magic very soon. She wanted it to be something amazing that would make everyone gaze in wonder—maybe light magic so he could create rainbows, or flying magic. She also couldn't wait for them to bond. When it happened, a strand of her long hair would turn the same pink and blue as Shimmer's mane, to show everyone they were partners for life. How cool would that be?

"I'm glad there haven't been any more tornadoes," said Aisha with a shiver.

"It is strange that we haven't found who was behind it," said Zara.

Phoebe stopped with a gasp. "That's it!" she exclaimed, throwing her hands up in the air. "I bet *that's* why Ms. Nettles was crying!"

"Why?" said Lily, looking puzzled.

"Because people suspect she was responsible!" Phoebe said dramatically. "Don't you see? This inspection is happening because people think *Ms. Nettles* is to blame!"

CHAPTER 2

"Phoebe!" Zara was shocked. "You can't go around saying stuff like that without any proof."

"You really can't," agreed Lily quickly. "Ms. Nettles loves the school. She'd never hurt it."

"Aha, but maybe she's just pretending to love it," said Phoebe excitedly. "Remember that a couple of years ago, the headteacher before Ms. Nettles did all sorts of things to try to harm the academy. Maybe Ms. Nettles has turned *evil*, just like her!"

"No, no, no!" said Aisha, looking shocked. "Ms. Nettles isn't evil!"

Phoebe raised her eyebrows and folded her arms. "She might be."

"Phoebe, it really can't be Ms. Nettles," said Zara. "We know the person responsible for the tornadoes is a man. Remember how we heard him shouting when Feather moved the tornado away from the academy. He said: *'You think you can stop me, but you can't.'*"

"Oh yes," said Phoebe, her excitement fading.

"I guess that Ms. Nettles might be upset because she's worried about the inspection," said Zara. "If she really was crying this morning like you say, then that may have been why."

"We should make sure the inspector thinks the school is perfect!" said Lily. "I don't want Ms. Nettles to get in trouble."

"Me neither," said Aisha. "Let's talk to the inspector and tell them how great all the teachers are—and what a great headteacher Ms. Nettles is."

"Definitely!" agreed Zara.

They reached the messy barn. There was hay all over the floor.

"We'd better get some brooms and start sweeping," said Aisha with a sigh.

"This will take ages," grumbled Phoebe.

Lily grinned. "Not if we use magic! Wait here. I'll go and get Feather!"

Feather's moving magic was very useful when it came to cleaning up. Soon the barn was filled with the sweet scent of burnt sugar—the smell of unicorn magic. Pink sparkles were fading in the

air, the loose hay was all in one big pile, and the other hay bales were piled up neatly.

"There!" said Feather happily.

"You're the best!" said Lily, hugging her. The yellow-violet-and-blue streak in her dark hair merged with Feather's mane.

Phoebe felt a flicker of envy. She really hoped she and Shimmer would bond soon. She could just imagine everyone paying attention to them. It would be fantastic!

With the barn cleaned up, Amethyst dorm set out for a ride around the grounds, sticking to the meadow to avoid the cross-country course. They cantered through the wildflowers and then let their unicorns splash in the sparkling stream.

As they rode back toward the stable yard, they saw a man in a suit getting out of a horse-drawn carriage at the school entrance. He was tall and thin with a stern face.

"Who's that?" said Aisha.

"I bet it's the inspector!" said Zara.

"But Ms. Tulip said he wouldn't be here until tomorrow," said Lily.

"I know, but it's got to be him. Look at the clues. He's carrying a suitcase and a clipboard, he's wearing a suit, and he's arriving in a carriage. He has to be someone official," said Zara.

"And he's already being nosy," said Phoebe as the man looked at the fountain in front of the school, frowned, and wrote something on his clipboard. "I wonder if Ms. Tulip knows he's here already."

"We should warn her!" said Zara.

They set off at a canter. When they reached the stables and told Ms. Tulip about the man, she looked worried. "It does sound like the inspector has arrived early. I hope he doesn't come out here yet. We're not done cleaning up."

"Don't worry. Feather will help!" said Lily.

Feather nodded eagerly.

While Feather used her magic, the rest of the students quickly groomed their unicorns. Then they went to their stables and made sure the straw beds were clean and fluffy and the hay nets full.

Ms. Tulip sighed in relief as she looked around the gleaming yard. "Well done, everyone. I think we're finally ready. Feather, you deserve a huge bucket of sky berries. Thank you! You must be tired after using so much magic."

Sky berries were unicorns' favorite food, and they were full of the vitamins they needed to stay healthy and keep their magic strong. Lily got Feather a bucket of the sweet juicy berries that grew behind the school. Then, leaving the unicorns to rest, the girls went in for lunch.

The students were eating salad and delicious baked potatoes with melted cheese when Ms.

Nettles brought the stranger into the dining room. Clapping her hands for silence, she introduced him.

"This is Mr. Long, everyone. He will be with us for a few days and is here to inspect the school. He will be sitting in on your lessons, and he may want to ask you some questions. I hope you will all be very helpful and answer as best you can."

Phoebe studied Mr. Long. With his dark suit, black tie, shiny black shoes, and sharp eyes, he almost looked like a villain. "I don't like him," she hissed to the others, while Ms. Nettles and Mr. Long sat down and the students started talking again. "He looks suspicious to me!"

"Me too," Aisha agreed.

Phoebe narrowed her eyes at the inspector. "I think he's up to something."

"Yes, inspecting the school!" said Zara, rolling her eyes. "Honestly, Phoebe. Next you'll be

imagining *he* was responsible for the tornadoes!"

Phoebe fell silent but watched the inspector carefully for the rest of lunch.

Afterward, they had Geography with Ms. Rivers. When they arrived at their classroom with Opal and Topaz dorms, they found Mr. Long already at the back of the room. He had his clipboard and a bunch of pens set out neatly on the desk in front of him.

"Good afternoon," he said.

"Good afternoon," everyone said politely. Exchanging looks, they all sat down.

The inspector walked over to Phoebe and Zara's desk. "Do you like being here at the academy?" he asked Phoebe.

"Oh yes, I love it!" Phoebe said. She couldn't wait to tell him how amazing the academy was. "It's the most exciting place!"

The inspector frowned. "Exciting?"

"Yes, there's always some huge drama happening!" Phoebe felt Zara kick her under the desk and glanced at her. Zara was looking panicked and giving tiny but quick shakes of her head.

"Drama?" the inspector echoed, his frown deepening. "So, you don't feel safe here?"

Phoebe's eyes widened. She hadn't meant that at all. "No, no, that isn't what—"

Just then, Ms. Rivers walked in.

"Quiet, please!" their teacher said, cutting across Phoebe's words.

"Students don't feel safe," the inspector muttered under his breath, making a note on his clipboard as he went back to his seat.

"Phoebe!" Zara hissed in horror. "Why did you say that?"

Phoebe felt awful. She hadn't meant to suggest that the students felt unsafe. Why hadn't she thought more carefully about what she was saying? What if Ms. Nettles got in trouble because of her?

I'll try to talk to him later, she thought, glancing back at the inspector, who was still scribbling notes. *I'll make sure he knows that I think the academy is the best school ever!*

CHAPTER 3

"Today we are going to be studying the thermal springs in the west of the island," Ms. Rivers announced. "They are in the mountains that are home to the golden-spotted phoenix."

There was the clatter of chair legs on the floor, and Mr. Long stood up. "Excuse me, Ms. Rivers, but I am a trained geologist. I happen to have visited the thermal springs. Would you like me to share some of my knowledge with the class?"

"Certainly," said Ms. Rivers politely. "I'm sure they'll all be very interested in what you have to say."

"Oh, we will! We really will!" Phoebe burst out.

She was hoping to make up for her earlier mistake by letting the inspector see how excited they all were about learning.

"Ms. Rivers, is it usual for students to be allowed to shout out in your class?" asked Mr. Long.

"No, of course not." Ms. Rivers frowned. "Phoebe, please remember to put your hand up."

Phoebe slid back into her seat. She hadn't made things better. If anything, she'd made them worse!

Mr. Long launched into a lengthy and boring description of how the hot springs were formed

and then showed the class how to greet the golden-spotted phoenix. "It's polite to bow from the waist, like this, while holding out your right hand at exactly this angle."

Mr. Long folded his thin frame in half while twisting his wrist to hold out his hand, with his fingers making a circle. Phoebe heard Spike and his friend Johan swallow snorts of laughter.

Mr. Long looked up sharply. "How rude!" he said. "I am surprised you allow behavior like this, Ms. Rivers." Picking up his clipboard, he made another note.

Ms. Rivers gave the boys a look that stopped them immediately. "Thank you, Mr. Long, for all that information. It was very interesting." Although Ms. Rivers's words were polite, Phoebe could tell from the tightness around her mouth and eyes that she was not happy at all.

When Geography ended, they went to get a

snack in the dining hall before going to a library session with Ms. Tansy, the librarian. Mr. Long walked with them, asking everyone questions as they went. Did they like the school? Did they feel safe?

"I'm going to talk to him," Phoebe told Zara.

"No, Phoebe!" Zara grabbed her arm.

Phoebe frowned. "Why not? I just want to make sure he knows students don't feel unsafe here. And I want to tell him how amazing the school is."

"Please don't," Zara begged. "You never think before you speak, and you'll only make things worse." She sounded so worried that Phoebe was surprised. She and Zara often teased each other—she would tell Zara she was too practical and Zara would tell her she was too dramatic—but this time Zara didn't sound as if she was teasing.

"Come on, let's get rainbow cakes," said Zara, pulling her into the dining hall.

Phoebe followed her, feeling confused and hurt. Did Zara really think she would make things worse if she spoke to the inspector?

"Where are the cakes today?" asked Aisha as they got to the counter.

"Didn't you hear?" said Lauren, who was from Opal dorm. "The kitchen ran out of flour. The delivery didn't come because Mount Inferno started rumbling overnight. The main road to the volcano has been closed while scientists investigate whether it's going to erupt."

"Really?" said Zara in surprise. She loved science, and she often read reports about the ancient volcano in the mountains behind the school. "But Mount Inferno has been dormant for over a hundred years."

"I overheard Ms. Rivers and Ms. Nettles

talking about it at lunchtime," said Spike, joining in the conversation. "No one knows why it's suddenly active again."

"Luckily no one lives on its slopes," said Zara. "And school's far enough away to be out of reach if Mount Inferno does erupt. The big danger will be to the villages nearby on the coast. Volcanic activity can affect the tides, and Mount Inferno is covered by a glacier—a huge river of ice. If it does erupt, the glacier will melt and cause horrible flooding."

"I hope it doesn't erupt!" said Lily.

"Maybe it's just going to rumble for a bit," said Aisha.

As everyone continued talking about the volcano, Zara looked at Phoebe. "You're being quiet."

"Am I?"

"Yes, normally if you heard news like this,

you'd be waving your arms, telling us we're all going to die!"

"Ha ha!" said Phoebe. "Very funny." But she didn't really feel like laughing for once. Zara's words from before were still stinging. While the others carried on talking about the volcano, she slipped away and went to the stables.

Shimmer whickered when he saw her. "Phoebe!"

"Hi, Shimmer," Phoebe muttered.

He blinked. "Are you okay?"

Phoebe shrugged.

"You're obviously not. What's the matter?" he asked, nuzzling her hands.

She sighed. "Do you think that I should be quieter?"

"What? No! Of course not!" Shimmer looked confused. "What are you talking about?"

Phoebe put her arms around his neck and

told him what had happened. "Zara said I'd make things worse if I spoke to the inspector. Would I make it worse, Shimmer?"

"No, of course not," Shimmer said loyally. He blew gently on her face. "You always say the right thing. You're perfect."

Phoebe loved him for being so supportive, but a tiny bit of her brain did wonder if Zara might be right. She sighed. "Maybe I do need to think more before I speak and not exaggerate as much," she said. "I did give the inspector the wrong idea."

"No!" said Shimmer quickly. "Please don't change. I like you just the way you are."

Phoebe smiled. "Thanks, Shimmer." She was very lucky to have him. He understood her in a way that no one else did. "I'd better go back in. We've got a library session now, and no doubt Mr. Long will be asking lots more questions. I don't like him. I hope he doesn't write a really

bad report on the school." She caught her breath. "What if he does and Ms. Nettles loses her job? Or what if it's so bad, the school closes and we're all sent home *forever*?"

Shimmer whickered as if he was laughing. "That's more like it!" He nudged her. "But even I think you're exaggerating now. Everyone knows how great Unicorn Academy is. One bad report won't be enough to close it."

Phoebe really hoped he was right.

CHAPTER 4

Ms. Tansy gathered them all together around the reading tree—a giant tree that grew through the floor of the library. She seemed nervous to have Mr. Long in the lesson with her and fiddled with her flower-shaped, yellow-rimmed glasses. "Right. Today, everyone, we're going to practice your researching skills by looking up famous inventors. I want you to start by trying to find out about Count Lysander Thornberry."

"I shall be fascinated to see what you find," Mr. Long said. "I know the count personally. He is a

fantastic scientist and an exceptional inventor. He was the first person to successfully combine magic and science to make a rain machine." A disapproving look crossed his face. "He might be vain, but his work is undeniably amazing."

Zara put her hand up. "I thought that Count Lysander Thornberry avoided people. How do you know him, Mr. Long?"

"We studied geology together before he became famous," said Mr. Long with a sniff. "The count was lucky enough to continue with his scientific work, becoming the famous inventor everyone knows today. I had to give up my research and get a paying job."

Phoebe raised her hand. "Mr. Long, if you studied geology, do you know much about volcanoes?"

"Phoebe, that's really not what we're doing

35

today," said Ms. Tansy, giving the inspector an anxious glance. "Today's lesson is about inventors, not volcanoes."

"No, no, it is quite all right, Ms. Tansy," said Mr. Long, his face losing some of its usual sternness. "Volcanoes are a particular interest of mine, and I completed several research papers on them before I became a school inspector. Do you have a question about volcanoes?" he asked Phoebe.

Phoebe nodded. "We heard that Mount Inferno's rumbling. How likely is it to erupt?"

"Now *that* is a very interesting question," Mr. Long said. He steepled his fingers beneath his chin. "Dormant volcanoes sometimes start to show signs of activity without erupting. The rumblings from Mount Inferno may be false alarms or they may signal that an eruption is about to happen."

"Will we be in danger here if it does erupt?" Tom from Topaz dorm asked.

"No, although the effects will be felt in other places, especially on the coast. A serious eruption will cause all sorts of problems." Mr. Long looked strangely excited. "If it does happen, it will be most interesting to study. Most interesting indeed!"

Phoebe watched his face curiously. He looked almost as if he *wanted* it to happen!

"Now, any other questions?" he asked.

"Why do you think it has become active again after all these years?" asked Zara.

"Well, there are several possibilities." Mr. Long started a boring speech about dormant volcanoes.

Zara listened carefully, but Phoebe soon gave up paying attention. Her thoughts returned

to earlier. Despite Shimmer asking her not to change, she wondered if she should try not to exaggerate so much. It was much more fun to make boring events into exciting stories, but she still felt bad she'd given Mr. Long the wrong idea about the school. She also disliked the way Zara hadn't trusted her to fix things. She sighed. Maybe she should stick to the facts more.

You know what? I'll try, she decided.

Phoebe's decision was quickly put to the test. As the day went on, more and more reports started coming in about the rumbling Mount Inferno. It seemed there had been several mini eruptions that were already causing problems.

"I spoke to my aunt, and she said there was such a high tide this afternoon that a rainbow-fountain

whale got stuck on the roof of her house," Spike said at lunch.

"And apparently the village next to ours has fallen down a huge crack that opened up in the road," countered Johan.

"And Lauren said that her cousin's house was under—" Phoebe broke off. She'd been about to say *underwater.* But really all Lauren had told her was that her cousin's family was evacuating from their village because of possible flooding. She sighed as she decided not to exaggerate the story. Telling only the facts was very boring.

"Under what?" said Zara.

"Nothing," muttered Phoebe, but as she saw everyone lose interest in her and start to look away, she suddenly couldn't stop herself. "Well, she said it was under a whole *sea* of water!" she said, her eyes widening. "Her family lost

everything—clothes, furniture, even the walls of the house were knocked down!"

She felt a rush of happiness as the others listened eagerly. Adding to the facts was so much more fun than sticking to them!

Ms. Nettles rose to her feet and waited until the room was silent. "Students, I need to talk to you about Mount Inferno. I believe you have heard that it has recently reawakened. But I want to assure you that help is being sent to those in need and you will be safe here at the academy."

Mr. Long unfolded his legs and stood up beside her. "Yes, Ms. Nettles. There is nothing to

worry about. However, this event happens once in a lifetime, and for that reason I propose that the students should go on a scientific trip to the coast. They can study the effects of the volcano becoming active again after so long."

Ms. Nettles blinked in surprise. "A field trip? But, Mr. Long, I cannot just interrupt the curriculum to let the students go camping."

"Why not?" said Mr. Long. "It will help improve their understanding of the island. I will choose an area that is safe, where they will be able to watch the effects of an active volcano. I suggest they study the earth tremors while recording the sea levels at high and low tide. I will, of course, be happy to join them and share my knowledge of volcanoes."

Ms. Nettles seemed lost for words. "I don't think this is a good idea, Mr. Long."

Mr. Long's eyebrows rose. "I'm sorry, Ms. Nettles? Are you saying you do not believe it is a good idea for your students to make the most of an exciting chance to learn?"

"Of course not!" said Ms. Nettles.

"Good," Mr. Long said. "Then the field trip will happen tomorrow."

He sat back down and picked up his clipboard.

Ms. Nettles took a deep breath and then looked around at the stunned students. "It appears there will be a field trip, after all," she said. "Lessons will be canceled to allow everyone to get ready. You can collect the food and camping equipment needed for yourselves and your unicorns after breakfast tomorrow."

The students broke into excited chatter as Ms. Nettles finished.

"A camping trip instead of lessons!" said Phoebe. "Awesome!"

"I wish we didn't have Mr. Long tagging along, though," said Lily. "I hate the way he keeps asking questions. It's like he only wants to find out bad things about the school."

"Let's stay out of his way," said Phoebe. "Just think—sleeping in tents, toasting marshmallows on the campfire." Her eyes shone. "And telling ghost stories at night!"

"I'll pack a flute so we can have some music," said Aisha. "But not my best one, in case it gets sandy."

"Studying the earth tremors and tide levels will be so interesting," said Zara excitedly. "I'll get some books on volcanoes from the library to read while we're there."

Phoebe rolled her eyes. "You *really* know how to have fun."

"It *is* fun," said Zara. "I'm also going to bring my detective notebook in case there's more to Mount Inferno coming to life than meets the eye."

"What do you mean?" asked Aisha, frowning.

Zara lowered her voice. "Don't you think it's strange that two really unusual environmental things happen within a few months of each other? First the purple tornadoes and now this. We know the tornadoes were caused by someone using bad magic. Maybe that same person has caused Mount Inferno to become active in order to harm the island some more."

"You really think they might be linked?" breathed Lily.

Zara nodded. "My uncle, the one who's a detective, says you should be very wary of coincidences. We should look out for clues, see if there are any links between the two events while

we're on the coast. Are you all in? Will you help me try to solve this mystery?"

"Definitely!" Phoebe, Lily, and Aisha said.

Phoebe felt excitement tingle through her. The field trip had suddenly gotten even more fun!

CHAPTER 5

The next morning, Ms. Nettles announced that the whole school was going to be allowed to travel to the coast using the magical map to save time. Everyone was very excited—the map was an exact model of the island that stood in the assembly hall and could be used to take people and their unicorns anywhere on the island.

Seated on their unicorns, Phoebe, Zara, Aisha, and Lily gathered around the map with the rest of the school. Their backpacks were filled with camping equipment and food. Zara's was heavier than everyone else's because she seemed to have packed half the library!

Phoebe felt like she was going to explode with excitement. "This is so awesome!" she exclaimed. "I can't wait to get there. Scoot over," she added to Zara. "I can't see the map."

The map was usually protected by a magical force field, but as the teachers and students crowded into the hall it shimmered and fell away. Ms. Nettles sat on her unicorn, Thyme, examining the west coast of the map and discussing it with Ms. Tulip, Ms. Rosemary, and Ms. Rivers. Mr. Long, dressed as usual in a dark suit, seemed to be arguing with them.

Nudging Zara, Phoebe said, "I've just thought of something. Why doesn't Mr. Long have a unicorn?"

"He didn't come to the academy when he was younger. He went to a different school, so

he's never had one," said Zara. "In fact, I heard Ms. Tulip telling Ms. Tansy that he can't even ride!"

"Ms. Tulip won't let him get away with that if he stays much longer!" said Lily with a grin. "She thinks everyone should ride!"

"Ms. Tulip is looking at him a lot," said Phoebe, observing the riding teacher, who kept glancing at Mr. Long. "Perhaps she's planning to get him on a unicorn while we're at the beach!"

Aisha giggled. "Or a donkey!"

Lily grinned. "Do you think he'll put on a swimsuit and go paddling in the sea while we're there?"

They all burst into giggles at the thought.

Ms. Nettles raised her hand for silence. "Quiet please, everyone. This is the first time I've used the map to transport the whole school. The magic should be strong enough, but for it to work,

everyone must hold hands. Don't let go or you will be left behind."

Phoebe took Zara's hand as Zara took Lily's. Phoebe was very glad she wasn't next to Mr. Long. She definitely wouldn't want to hold hands with him!

Ms. Nettles cleared her throat. "Are we all ready? Aisha, you're not holding on to anyone."

"Sorry," said Aisha, who was taking off her backpack. "I think I've forgotten something important."

Ms. Nettles sighed. "If it's your flute, my dear, then I can see it sticking out of your bag."

"Phew! Thanks, Ms. Nettles."

Phoebe grinned and squeezed Aisha's hand as she took it. Aisha squeezed back.

Ms. Nettles placed her free hand on the magical map. Speaking in a loud, clear voice, she said, "Take us all to the west coast."

At first, Phoebe thought that the humming noise she could hear was Aisha, but then she realized it was the magical map. A wind sprang up, snatching Phoebe's hair and whipping at her cheeks. Zara's and Aisha's hands were ripped from hers as the wind lifted Shimmer up. Lights flashed, and then they were spinning so fast that it was impossible to see.

"Eeeee!" squealed Phoebe, grabbing Shimmer's mane. Her long braids flew around her face as she spun through the air. Then, suddenly, she was falling. Her stomach dipped as the ground rushed up to meet her, but Shimmer landed safely with only a soft *bump*.

"Wow!" said Phoebe, catching her breath as Zara, Aisha, and Lily landed beside her on their unicorns. Around her, unicorns, students, and teachers were landing with gentle thuds. They were on a grassy cliff top. Below, red rocks fell away to golden sand beneath. In the distance, Phoebe could see the blue sea.

"Isn't it beautiful?" said Aisha.

"Oh, it's so good to smell the sea again!" said Lily, sniffing happily. She and her mom lived on the east coast.

There was a louder *bump* and a shout behind them. Phoebe turned and had to cover her mouth

with her hands to stop herself from laughing. Mr. Long had arrived and landed facedown, with his legs crumpled beneath him. His face was berry beetle red as he scrambled up and brushed the grass from his dark suit.

"Ms. Nettles!" he said. "You have brought us to the wrong place. I remember saying that we would camp on the beach. We shall be recording the level of the tide at all hours of the day and night, and I don't want to have to walk too far."

Ms. Nettles sucked in her cheeks. "Thank you, Mr. Long, but while I am headteacher, the safety of my students is my responsibility. Given the unusual fluctuations in the tide, it would not be safe for them to camp out on the beach. Their tents could easily be washed away by an exceptionally high tide. Everyone can access the beach by one of several cliff paths." She held Mr. Long's eye until a pink flush spread up his neck.

"Very well," he said. "You may continue to decide the students' campsites."

Ms. Nettles pursed her mouth.

Ooh, she really doesn't like him, Phoebe thought, reading her expression.

After a moment, the headteacher nodded. "The teachers will camp here. Each dormitory will pitch its tents at a different site in a line along the cliffs. Amethyst dorm, you will have the campsite farthest away. Ms. Rosemary, will you show them where to go, please?"

"Of course," said Ms. Rosemary. She patted her unicorn and smiled at the girls. "Come on, then, follow me."

They rode until the cliff began to slope down, and they spotted a cluster of stone houses above the beach. Ms. Rosemary pulled up to a spot that was protected by bushes and a crumbling stone wall. "This can be your campsite. Set up your

tents. I will ride down into the village and tell them you're camping here."

"Let's pitch the tents by the wall so we have some protection from the wind," said Zara as Ms. Rosemary rode away.

There were three tents. Phoebe and Zara were sharing one, Aisha and Lily were sharing another, and there was one for their things. They pitched them with their backs to the wall and then made a fire of sticks, using rocks to stop it from spreading when it was lit. Ms. Rosemary returned at a gallop, her face flushed.

"Girls, I need your help! The village was flooded last night after an unusually high tide that came halfway up the cliff."

"But Mr. Long said

there wouldn't be flooding here," said Aisha in surprise.

"I know, but clearly he was wrong. I need you to come with me and lend a hand with cleaning up."

The girls jumped on their unicorns.

"An unusually high tide that no one expected!" exclaimed Zara as they headed toward the houses. "Another unusual environmental event." Her eyes gleamed. "There could be something suspicious about it. Keep a lookout for clues, everyone!"

CHAPTER 6

As they cantered into the village, Phoebe felt like a superhero, swooping in and coming to the villagers' rescue. However, she quickly discovered that cleaning up after a flood was not exciting in the least. The first thing that hit her was the smell coming from the piles of rotting seaweed. The doors of buildings were thrown open as people wearing rain boots shoveled water out of their houses. There were piles of stuff everywhere. Soggy bedding, clothes, and rugs were all tangled up with seaweed and shells and items that had been swept into the surrounding fields.

The villagers were very happy to have the girls' help. Lily and Feather set to work immediately, using Feather's magic to help get the heaviest items that had floated away. The other girls

grabbed brooms and started to sweep out the water, while their unicorns picked things up with their teeth and hung them out to dry.

Phoebe was glad to help, but she thought that cleaning up was pretty boring.

"I wish I'd discovered my magic," Shimmer said with a sigh as they paused to watch Feather. Feather was using her magic to carry a cart back from the fields.

Phoebe couldn't have agreed more. Doing magic would be much more fun than sweeping and wringing the water out of wet clothes. "How about we go to that ruined cottage on the cliff path over there? I can see some things that need retrieving, and at least we'll get away from the smell for a while."

"Okay," said Shimmer eagerly.

Phoebe climbed onto his back and they

cantered across the grass. The cottage roof had fallen in a while ago, and moss clung to the stone walls. Clearly, no one had lived in it for a long time, and as Phoebe and Shimmer got closer, they saw that the walls were just an empty shell. The grass surrounding it was scattered with objects that had been swept there by the flood water—buckets, flowerpots, baskets. . . .

Phoebe jumped off Shimmer and started collecting anything she could carry. As she got close to the doorway, something moved in the shadows inside the ruin. She gasped and jumped as a seagull flew up into the air with a loud cry.

Phoebe took a trembling breath. It was just a bird. She picked up some more flowerpots and returned to Shimmer. He was holding a spade in his teeth.

"Let's take this stuff back to the village," she said. "This cottage feels creepy."

When they got back, Zara came riding up on Moonbeam. "Guess what? I've been talking to some of the villagers, and a few of them mentioned seeing a stranger hanging around the village in the last few days. They all remembered him for his clothes—he was dressed in a black suit with a long coattail and a tall hat. He sounds suspicious, doesn't he?"

"Ooh yes. He could be the culprit who caused the purple tornadoes. And he might be responsible for the floods," said Shimmer.

Moonbeam nodded. "It feels like someone has been doing dark magic around here. The air is thicker—heavier," she said.

"I feel it, too!" said Phoebe. She couldn't actually feel anything different about the air, but

it was great that Moonbeam was adding to the drama.

"We shouldn't jump to conclusions," said Zara quickly. "We need evidence, but the sighting of this man is definitely a possible clue. The villagers I spoke to said he was hanging around the beach and walking near the old ruined cottage."

"We were just there," said Phoebe.

"Did you see anything?" Zara asked eagerly.

"Well, it did feel creepy, and I saw something move in the shadows," said Phoebe.

Shimmer nodded. "It made Phoebe jump really high!"

Seeing the look of enthusiasm on Zara's face, Phoebe couldn't help adding to her story. "It might have been a person. In fact, I really think it might have been a man!"

Zara gasped. "We need to investigate this.

Come on!" Moonbeam whinnied and set off for the cottage.

As Shimmer followed them, Phoebe felt a flutter of guilt. She hadn't really seen a man. She knew it had been just a bird. She hadn't thought Zara would be so excited.

Zara and Moonbeam went into the ruins of the cottage.

"Wait, Shimmer!" Phoebe said as he went to follow them inside. "Do you think I should tell Zara I was making up that stuff about a man?" she whispered.

Shimmer looked surprised. "No. Why?"

"Well, there wasn't really one, and now Zara thinks there was and—"

She was interrupted by a shout from Zara. "Look at this!" Zara said, waving something at them.

Phoebe and Shimmer went closer. Zara was holding a pale gray button with an unusual sheen, stamped with a two-headed serpent wrapped around a strange symbol. "I found this inside. It must have come from the mystery man's clothes. Oh, this is SO exciting. It's a real clue! Well done, Phoebe! I wouldn't have found it if you hadn't spotted the man!"

"Well . . . um . . . ," Phoebe started to say.

"Beware the tall, cloaked stranger," Moonbeam said dreamily.

Zara looked around. "What?"

Moonbeam blinked. "Sorry. I don't know why I just said that."

Zara rolled her eyes. "Moonbeam, concentrate! This is serious stuff. A suspect has been here, and this button may have come off his clothes. We should stake out this place tonight in case he's using it to cause trouble for the island. That's when he'll do something, under the cover of darkness when there's no one else around." She rushed on. "We'll need somewhere to hide." She looked around. "How about that shed? We can hide behind the walls. Let's go and tell the others! Operation Catch the Suspect is on!"

She jumped on Moonbeam and they galloped away.

Phoebe's heart dropped. "Whoops," she said, looking at Shimmer.

"Don't worry," he said, nuzzling her. "Zara will never know you didn't really see a man."

"But I feel bad because she's so excited about it," said Phoebe. "And now we're all going on a stakeout to watch for someone I never saw, who might not even be anywhere near here, instead of having fun camping!" She bit her lip. "Oh, Shimmer! What have I done?"

CHAPTER 7

It was getting late when they returned to the village. Everything was looking much tidier, and Ms. Rosemary sent the girls back to their camp. All Zara, Aisha, and Lily talked about on the way was the mysterious man and the button. Phoebe got quieter and quieter.

When they reached the tents, the unicorns trotted back down to the beach to roll around on the sand and paddle in the sea. Phoebe went to the storage tent to get Shimmer some sky berries for when he got back.

Lily followed her. "Are you all right, Phoebe? You don't seem yourself."

Phoebe wondered whether to tell Lily the truth. She loved Shimmer, but she wasn't sure if she should keep lying. Teasing Zara and telling a few small stories was one thing. But letting her plan a midnight stakeout and getting her hopes up that they were actually going to catch the man doing dark magic was another. She decided to confess. "I've . . . I've done something really bad, Lily."

"What?" Lily asked in concern.

Taking a deep breath, Phoebe told her everything.

"Oh, Phoebe," said Lily, shaking her head.

"What should I do?" Phoebe muttered.

"You have to own up," said Lily. "Zara will be upset, but she'll get over it. You can't keep lying to her."

Phoebe nodded, knowing she was right. "I'd better go and tell her now."

Lily put an arm around her. "You'll feel much better once you've confessed. I'll finish up here and feed all the unicorns. You go and see Zara. Good luck!"

"Thanks." Once Phoebe made her mind up about something, she liked to do it immediately. She went to her and Zara's tent and lifted the flap. Zara was inside, writing neat notes in her detective notebook, frowning in concentration. She smiled when she saw Phoebe.

"Um, Zara," said Phoebe, her heart beating fast. "Can I talk to you?"

Zara looked up. "Can it wait? I want to draw a picture of the button so we have a record of it in case we lose it. I'm going to see if the man left any more clues while we're on the stakeout."

Phoebe's tummy twisted into a knot as she ducked inside. "Erm, about this stakeout. I need to tell you something. . . ."

As Phoebe confessed, Zara's smile faded.

"It was all made-up?" Her voice rose. "You didn't see a man there? You *lied* to me!" She threw her notebook down.

Unhappiness curled through Phoebe as she saw the hurt in Zara's eyes. "I'm sorry."

"So this button isn't a clue. It probably doesn't have anything to do with him!" said Zara.

"It might," Phoebe pointed out. "The villagers did say they had seen a man walking near there.

It's just *I* didn't actually see him in the cottage—
or at all."

"I can't believe you lied to me, Phoebe!" Zara
said angrily. "Did you think it was funny to trick
me? The island is in danger. It's not a joke!
I thought you really wanted to help solve the
mystery."

"I do and I am sorry. I just said that stuff about
the man without thinking."

"Well, maybe you *should* think in the future!"
Zara exclaimed. "Just go away!"

Phoebe backed away, and the tent flap closed.
She almost never cried, but now she could feel
tears stinging her eyes. She hated knowing she
had hurt and upset one of her best friends.

She crept off to find Shimmer. He was eating
the sky berries Lily had left for him.

"Hi, Phoebe," he said through a mouthful of
berries. "We just had the best water fight in the

ocean. I'm so good at splashing, and guess what? We saw Mr. Long down by the water. I almost got him with a big splash!" He saw her face and broke off. "What's the matter?"

"Zara is really upset with me," Phoebe confessed. "I told her that I made up the story about seeing the man."

Shimmer looked astonished. "What did you do that for?"

"I felt bad that she was planning the stakeout and everything based on what I said I saw. Now she's really angry and not talking to me."

Shimmer huffed. "Oh, she's just being silly and making a big deal out of nothing. Ignore her."

Phoebe stroked his mane and climbed onto his back. It was lovely of him to be on her side, but she was the one who was wrong, not Zara.

Shimmer nudged her. "Hey, should we go to the beach? Then you can see how good I am

at splashing. If I stamp my hoof like this"—
Shimmer struck the ground with a hoof—"POW!
The water explodes everywhere!"

Phoebe caught something bright pink
flickering around Shimmer's hoof. Her eyes
widened. "Shimmer, what was that?"

"What?" he said.

"I saw a spark fly up. Do it again, Shimmer.
Stamp your hoof!"

"Are you tricking me?" he said suspiciously.

"No!"

Shimmer half-heartedly banged his hoof on the
ground, looking as if he didn't believe Phoebe.

"Harder!" she urged him.

Shimmer smacked his hoof to the floor with
a *bang.* "Like that? Whoa!" A tiny bolt of magic
shot from his hoof, crisscrossing over the grass
and hitting a stone. *CRACK!* The stone shattered,
leaving a strong, sugary smell hanging in the air.

Phoebe gasped. "You've found your magic! Oh, Shimmer!" She flung her arms around him and then looked over at the shattered rock. "But . . . what type of magic is it?"

"I don't know!" Shimmer said in shock.

He stamped his hoof again. With a crack, a bolt of magic flew across the grass, hitting a boulder and splitting it in half.

"Wow! That's powerful!" yelped Phoebe in excitement.

Shimmer exploded a bucket next, almost soaking them both as the water spilled out.

Phoebe squealed. "Stop it! You're going to wreck the camp! You'd better stop practicing, at least until we've worked out what kind of magic you've got."

"All right," said Shimmer, a little sadly. "It is hard. I feel really tired now."

Phoebe leaped off Shimmer's back. "Wait here. I'll go and tell the others!" Phoebe said, and buzzing with excitement, she raced to the tents to tell her friends the news.

CHAPTER 8

"Go away!" said Zara again when Phoebe stuck her head inside her tent. She was sitting cross-legged on her sleeping bag, talking to Lily and Aisha.

Phoebe still felt bad about before, but Shimmer getting his magic was far more important than any argument. "Shimmer's found his magic!" she exclaimed.

"What?" said Lily.

"It's awesome!" Phoebe rushed on. "But we don't know exactly what it is. He keeps exploding things!"

"Are you joking?" Zara gave her a withering look. "Phoebe, have you seriously not learned anything today? Making stuff up just isn't funny."

"But I'm not making this up!" Phoebe said. "Shimmer was messing around, banging his hoof on the ground, when suddenly a mini bolt of magic flew out and a stone exploded. Then he shattered a boulder—a whole boulder—and a water bucket! It was incredible."

Zara studied her hands.

"Phoebe, be honest. Is this just another of your stories?" asked Lily, their eyes meeting.

"No, it's the truth," said Phoebe. "Cross my heart and hope to die. Come and see!"

Aisha and Lily got to their feet. "Are you coming, Zara?" Lily asked.

Zara sighed. "All right, I'll come. But you'd better be telling the truth this time, Phoebe."

They walked outside and went to Shimmer. He'd called the other unicorns over.

"Okay, everyone, are you going to watch my magic?" he said. "Stand back. It's *very* powerful," he bragged.

Dramatically, Shimmer brought his hoof down on the ground. Nothing happened. He tried again, and all he managed to do was to move some dirt with his hoof. The other unicorns snorted and looked at each other.

Zara exclaimed in disbelief and stomped back to her tent. "I knew it!" she called over her shoulder. "I just knew you were lying, Phoebe!"

"Phoebe!" Lily said in frustration. "I really believed you. How could you upset Zara again?"

"Wait, Zara!" Aisha called. She and Lily ran after her. Their unicorns all went too.

Phoebe fought back tears as she watched Aisha and Lily put their arms around Zara.

"Phoebe, I'm so sorry." Shimmer's eyes were huge. "I think I must have worn myself out using my magic before, and now I've let you down and made you look like a liar in front of everyone."

"It's all right." Phoebe buried her face in Shimmer's mane so that he couldn't see how upset she was. "It's not your fault, it's mine. I do always make things up. I don't blame Zara and the others for not believing me this time." She shook her head. "I tried to change before but didn't manage it. From now on, I really am going to tell the truth. If I start exaggerating, then you must stop me and not encourage me." Phoebe looked Shimmer in the eyes. "If we're going to make good guardians of Unicorn Island, then we have to bring out the best in each other, not the worst."

Shimmer nodded. "You're right, Phoebe. I love the way you tell stories and make everything so exciting, but people need to be able trust us. Especially now that I have my magic, whatever it is."

"I'll help you find out. We'll start tomorrow." Phoebe cuddled up closer to Shimmer. "I love you, Shimmer. You're the best unicorn ever."

"I love you too, Phoebe," he said, nuzzling her.

Shimmer lay down, and Phoebe snuggled under his mane, cuddling it like a soft, silky blanket. It had been a long day, and she suddenly realized how tired she was. She was just dozing off to sleep when Aisha and Lily came out to find her.

"Are you okay?" Aisha asked softly.

Phoebe nodded sleepily. "I think I'm going to sleep under the stars tonight with Shimmer."

"But you haven't had any dinner," said Aisha.

"I'm okay," said Phoebe. She didn't want to go to camp and face Zara. "I'll have a big breakfast in the morning."

"Wait here!" said Lily. She and Aisha hurried away and came back with Phoebe's dinner of sandwiches and an apple.

"Thanks," Phoebe said.

"See you in the morning," they said.

She smiled as they crept away. At least Aisha and Lily didn't hate her. The hard knot inside her began to loosen. She ate her cheese sandwiches, shared the crusts and her apple with Shimmer, then closed her eyes, and seconds later she was fast asleep.

Phoebe woke at dawn to the cry of seagulls as they swooped overhead. Sitting up, she ran a hand through her tangled hair.

"Morning," Shimmer whickered, his breath warm on her cheek.

"Morning," said Phoebe, stretching.

Shimmer got to his feet. "I feel much better after a good night's sleep. I have a ton of energy. I bet my magic will work again now."

Moving away from Phoebe, he stamped a hoof. Sparks fizzed up into the air, and a nearby rock shattered into hundreds of pieces.

Phoebe clapped with delight. "That's awesome, Shimmer. If only we knew exactly what magic it is. I wish we could ask Zara about it. She's really good at scientific stuff like that."

"There's Zara now," said Shimmer, nodding toward the coastal path. Phoebe followed his gaze and saw Zara riding Moonbeam down to the beach.

"I think I might go after her and try apologizing again," she said.

"Let's both go," said Shimmer. Phoebe jumped onto his back, and they cantered after Zara and Moonbeam. They caught up to them on the beach. Zara had dismounted, and both she and Moonbeam were staring out at the distant sea. It was really far out, leaving a huge amount of bare, damp sand. Slipping from Shimmer's back, Phoebe ran over to stand beside Zara.

"Zara, I'm sorry," she said. "I really didn't mean to upset you yesterday. I shouldn't have lied about seeing the man. It was thoughtless of me, and I'm going to try to tell the facts from now on and not make stuff up. But I wasn't lying about Shimmer, he really does have his magic."

Zara glanced at her. "Really?"

"Yes, it didn't work yesterday because he'd tired himself out. It's working again now." Phoebe flicked her hair. "I can show you—"

Zara gasped. "Phoebe! Your hair." Reaching out, she lifted a long strand of pink and pale blue. "You and Shimmer have bonded!"

"We have?" Phoebe squinted to look. "Shimmer, we've bonded!" she squealed, kissing him.

"It must have happened in the night," he whickered, nuzzling her back.

"Aw! Well done, you two." Despite the

argument from yesterday, Zara looked really happy for them. "So I guess that means you really were telling the truth? Shimmer actually *did* find his magic?"

"Yes, I did," said Shimmer. "Watch this." He flicked his hoof, and a bolt of magic scorched across the beach, hitting a jagged rock that exploded. Zara's mouth dropped open.

"Wow!" she breathed. "Energy magic! That means you can create bolts or balls of pure magical energy. My great-aunt's unicorn has energy magic. No wonder you tired yourself out

yesterday when you found it. It's very powerful."

"Zara, something doesn't feel right," said Moonbeam uneasily, staring out over the sand. "The air feels wrong."

Phoebe followed her gaze. "The sea is really far out, isn't it?"

"Yes," said Zara, her forehead crinkling. "It shouldn't be. According to the tide times, it should be halfway in by now."

"It's coming," Moonbeam muttered.

"It doesn't look like it is," said Zara, giving her a strange look. "It looks like it's going out."

"Beware the man with the cloak," Moonbeam said.

"The man with the cloak! Why are you being weird again, Moonbeam?" Zara demanded.

Moonbeam blinked. "I . . . I don't know. I'm sorry. I don't know what I meant."

"Hey, everyone," Shimmer interrupted. "It's gone really quiet all of a sudden. There are no birds, and I can't see the ocean anymore."

Phoebe realized he was right. There was no sign of any water at all now, just sand as far as the eye could see. "What's happening?"

Zara's face paled. "Oh no! I've read about this. It happens before a tsunami hits."

"What's a tsunami?" said Shimmer.

Zara gulped. "A giant tidal wave that sweeps away anything and anyone in its path!"

CHAPTER 9

"Quick! We've got to warn the others!" Phoebe cried.

Phoebe and Zara leaped onto their unicorns and thundered back up the cliff path, yelling loudly to wake their friends up.

"What's all the noise about?" Aisha said as she and Lily stumbled from their tents, pulling on clothes.

"Phoebe! Your hair!" Lily gasped. "You've bonded with Shimmer."

"Yes, and he really does have his magic—energy

magic—but that's not important right now," Phoebe said. "What matters is that everyone is in danger!"

The words tumbled out of Zara and Phoebe as they explained about the sea.

"What can we do?" asked Aisha.

"Nothing," said Lily worriedly. "There is absolutely nothing that can stop a tsunami. The only thing to do is get as far away as possible."

"We need to warn everyone before it hits," said Phoebe frantically.

"Let's go!" said Lily.

"Wait!" cried Zara. She pointed at Lily. "There *is* something that can stop a tsunami! I read about it in one of the books last night. Scientists have a new theory. There are special types of sound waves called acoustic-gravity waves that can move really fast through the ocean. And scientists

believe that if these waves of energy could be shot right into a tsunami, they could break it up and weaken it. They haven't found a way to do it yet, it's just a theory."

"Well, how will that help us?" said Phoebe. "If the scientists don't know how to fire these acoustic-gravity waves into a tsunami, then what can *we* do?"

"Use magic!" said Zara, her eyes gleaming. "If Shimmer shoots the tsunami with pure balls of energy, it might just have the same effect as firing acoustic-gravity waves. It may break up the tsunami before it hits the coast."

"Could it work?" asked Lily.

"I don't know. But it's our only chance." Zara looked at Shimmer. "Would you try, Shimmer?"

He glanced uncertainly at Phoebe. "Do you think I can do this?"

Phoebe stroked his cheek. "I think you can do anything you set your mind to."

Shimmer stood a little taller. "Then I'll try!" he declared.

"You'd better be quick!" whinnied Moonbeam.

Phoebe gasped as she looked out to sea and saw a huge blue wall of water rolling toward them. It seemed to blot out half the sky. *We're doomed,* she thought, but then she realized she had a very important job to do and had to stay calm. She didn't speak her thought out loud. "You can do this, Shimmer," she told him fiercely. "I know you can."

"We believe in you, Shimmer!" cried Zara, lifting her voice above the thundering of the water.

"Try, please try!" begged Lily as their unicorns whinnied encouragement.

Shimmer reared up and stamped both front

hooves on the ground as hard as he could. A massive blue ball of energy exploded from his hooves and shot through the air toward the incoming tsunami. Phoebe held her breath as it smashed into it.

"Again, Shimmer!" she cried.

Zara whooped. "We're combining magic and science. This is amazing! Go, Shimmer!"

Shimmer stamped his hooves over and over again. Huge balls of energy bowled through the air, hitting the tidal wave one after the other. Shimmer's sides heaved and his legs began to buckle, and still he kept going.

"The wave is slowing down!" yelled Lily. "I'm sure of it."

"Keep going!" shouted Aisha.

The gigantic wave had slowed but was still approaching. The thundering was so loud,

Phoebe could hardly hear herself think. Her heart thumped for the villagers who wouldn't have time to run for their lives, for her school friends on the side of the cliff, for the teachers and all the unicorns. Shimmer was their only hope. Her throat tightened. "Keep trying, Shimmer! Don't give up!" she begged. "You can beat the wave!"

The wave peaked, curling high with white froth.

It's over, thought Phoebe. But . . . wait . . . was

that a wobble? The giant wave teetered. Gaps appeared in it, holes breaking through the thick blue wall as the water splashed back into the sea and the wave slowly shrunk.

"Do it again!" gasped Phoebe, giving Shimmer a kiss. His body trembled with tiredness but he cracked his hoof down on the ground, sending his largest bolt of pure magic spinning into the center of the wave. The wave folded over.

As the wave teetered, a man's voice could be heard bellowing furiously above the fading roar of the water. "You think you can stop me, but you can't. I will return, and next time, chaos will win."

The tsunami collapsed into the sea, shooting a jet of water into the air.

"We did it!" Shimmer panted.

The ocean calmed. Shimmer swayed,

exhausted from using so much magic. Hearing shouts, Phoebe looked around. The teachers and other students were galloping toward them, and Mr. Long was running from the opposite direction, from the coastal path by the village.

"Is everyone safe?" asked Ms. Nettles as Thyme skidded to a halt on the grass.

Behind her, all the students were yelling.

"Did you see that wave?"

"It was huge!"

"I thought it was going to hit us!"

"What is going on here?" yelled Mr. Long. His face was pale and his suit was wrinkled and sandy. "What happened to the tsunami?"

"It was Shimmer! He saved us!" cried Zara. "He's got energy magic!"

"It's thanks to Zara's science knowledge—

97

she got Shimmer to use his magic to stop the tsunami, and it worked!" said Phoebe. She and Zara hugged in delight.

Mr. Long's mouth gaped open. For once, he was at a loss for words.

Ms. Nettles also looked completely shocked. "Shimmer stopped the tsunami?"

Zara nodded and smiled at Phoebe. "Tell everyone what happened, Phoebe!"

Phoebe beamed as everyone turned to her. She was center stage, and this time she didn't even have to make anything up. The truth was exciting enough!

As she described their adventure, Ms. Nettles's glasses rattled so hard they almost slid off her nose. "You saved everyone!" she said. "Thank you, Shimmer, for facing danger head-on to protect your friends and our island. And thank

you, Phoebe, for being there for him. He would not have had enough energy if you hadn't been by his side, believing in him."

"I couldn't have done it either if my friends hadn't been there," said Phoebe, smiling around at her dorm.

Everyone ran forward to congratulate Amethyst dorm. Mr. Long hung back awkwardly until Ms. Tulip went over and helped brush his suit down. Then Phoebe saw him start to smile and talk to her.

Finally, Ms. Nettles shooed everyone away. "Shimmer needs to rest, and the girls should, too. I declare this a day off for everyone. We will spend our time at the beach."

"What about the tsunami and the man's voice we heard? It was definitely the same one that we heard in the purple tornado," Zara said.

"Leave that to us," said Ms. Nettles firmly. "We will look into this."

As the teachers left, Phoebe fed Shimmer handfuls of sky berries until he began to get his energy back. "I'm so proud of you!"

"I'm proud of you too," he countered. "And guess what I've learned today? Being center stage is so much nicer when you've actually worked

hard to get there, especially if you do it with a friend. Defeating the tsunami was hard, but it was also the best thing I've ever done. I couldn't have beaten it without your help. We're great partners! We'll be guardians together forever, and that feels amazing."

Phoebe smiled. "I feel the same."

"Come on, you two." Zara ran over. "Ms. Nettles said we can have our breakfast on the beach. Sausages cooked on the grill!"

A short while later, Phoebe and the others were sitting on towels on the sand, finishing their sausage sandwiches, while their unicorns splashed in the ocean. "This is the nicest breakfast ever," Phoebe said with a contented sigh. "Food always tastes better when it's cooked and eaten outside." She looked around at her friends. "Look, I just want to apologize to you all, but especially to Zara, for telling stories. I promise not to tell a story ever again!"

"Don't do that!" Aisha was alarmed. "We all love your stories."

"Yes, don't change," Lily added. "We really do like you just the way you are."

Zara grinned. "Just promise me you won't make up stories about important things like suspects and clues anymore, okay?"

"Okay," said Phoebe. "I promise I won't do that and I promise that I'll always tell the facts when it matters." She felt a rush of happiness. Her friends were the best!

"You know, I keep thinking about that voice in the tsunami," said Lily with a shiver.

"I will return," Phoebe mimicked in a spooky voice.

"Who is he and what's he going to do next time?" said Aisha.

"We've got to try to find out." Zara pulled the button out of her pocket. "I wonder if this *is* a clue. After all, even though you didn't see the strange man in the ruined cottage, Phoebe, the villagers said they'd seen him near there. This could be from his clothes."

"I bet it is," said Phoebe. "And I bet his was the voice we heard."

They passed the button around.

"I wonder why he wants to harm the island," said Aisha.

"I don't know, but it's a mystery I plan to solve." Zara's eyes shone. "Who's with me?"

"Me!" they all shouted back.

"We'll work out who the mystery man is and solve the crime!" whooped Phoebe. "Amethyst dorm is the best!"

"Look at Shimmer," said Lily suddenly. The unicorns were playing in the surf. Shimmer was stamping his hooves, sending mini bolts of magic bouncing across the water, soaking the other unicorns as the magic exploded in the waves.

"Yay! Water fight!" shouted Phoebe, jumping up and running down to the water. She squealed with delight as Shimmer shot a ball of energy into the water, soaking her from her head to her toes. She flung her arms around his neck. "Do you know something?"

"What?" he said.

"You're not only the best unicorn ever with the most awesome power. You are also, one hundred percent, my best friend."

Shimmer whinnied happily.

Phoebe beamed and shouted to the others. "Come along, all of you! It's not just fun in here, it's *magic*!"

The others leaped to their feet and raced across the sand to join the unicorns in the sparkling waves.

A terrible heat wave is coming to
Unicorn Island! Can Zara and Moonbeam
save the island before it's too late?

Read on for a peek at the next book in the
Unicorn Academy Nature Magic series!

"We won!" Zara punched the air as her unicorn, Moonbeam, galloped across the dry grass and plunged into Sparkle Lake.

"Yay!" Moonbeam kicked up her hooves, showering them both with the glittering water.

Zara pushed her straight brown hair away from her face. "Hurry up, slowpokes!" she called to her friends. "It's lovely and cool!"

With whoops of delight, Phoebe, Lily, and Aisha galloped into the lake on their unicorns Shimmer, Feather, and Silver.

"It was so hot and stuffy this morning in class,

I honestly thought I was going to die. I think we should ask Ms. Rosemary if we can have afternoon lessons in the lake," said Phoebe, pushing her long blond braids over her shoulders. "It would be awesome!"

Zara laughed. "Yep, because she'll *definitely* agree to that!"

It was the middle of the summer, and Unicorn Island was suffering from a heat wave. At first, Zara and her friends in Amethyst dormitory had loved the long hot days and nights. But after several weeks of soaring temperatures, it was getting too hot. The grass had dried to a yellow crisp, and the flowers and plants had all wilted. The fountain was now half its height, and the lake had shrunk, leaving a rim of cracked dried mud around the edge.

The unicorns splashed around, kicking water at each other with their hooves.

Lily leaned forward and whispered in Feather's ear. Suddenly the lake began to ripple. Zara smelled the sweet sugary scent of magic and saw sparkles bubbling up through the water from Feather's hooves. The ripples grew stronger until the water rose in a tall, glittering wave. It arched high over Zara, Phoebe, and Aisha. Zara held her breath, expecting to be soaked.

CRACK! More magical sparkles fizzed in the air and the wave exploded, raining shimmering droplets down on everyone.

Zara laughed, enjoying the cool mist falling on her face and hair.

Lily, Phoebe, and Aisha clapped and cheered. "Go, Feather and Shimmer!"

Zara clapped, too, but she couldn't help feeling a little bit envious. She knew Lily's unicorn, Feather, had created the wave with her special moving magic and Phoebe's unicorn,

Shimmer, had broken it with his energy magic. When would Moonbeam discover her magic? The unicorns usually found their special magical powers during their first year at the academy. Those who didn't had to stay on for a second year with their partners.

"He's coming back," Moonbeam whispered.

Zara leaned over her neck. "Who's coming back?" she asked, wondering what Moonbeam was talking about.

"He is," said Moonbeam dreamily.

"But who?" said Zara. "Who are you talking about?" She felt a prickle of frustration. Moonbeam often went off into daydreams. "What do you mean, Moonbeam?"

MerMiCORns

Swim into a new series!

MerMiCORns — 1

Sparkle Magic

Sudipta Bardhan-Quallen

Mermicorns are part unicorn, part mermaid, and totally magical!

New friends. New adventures.
Find a new series ... just for you!

ISADORA MOON

For ballerina and fairy and vampire lovers

MAGIC ON THE MAP

For adventurers

UNICORN ACADEMY

For unicorn lovers

PUPPY PIRATES

For dog lovers

PuRRmaids

For mermaid and cat lovers

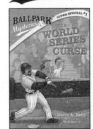
BALLPARK Mysteries

For sports fans

1220b

 rhcbooks.com

⌒ Collect all the books in the ⌒ Horse Diaries series!

Elska

CATHERINE HAPKA
Illustrated by RUTH SANDERSON

Bell's Star

ALISON HART
Illustrated by RUTH SANDERSON

Koda

PATRICIA HERMES
Illustrated by RUTH SANDERSON

Luna

CATHERINE HAPKA
Illustrated by RUTH SANDERSON

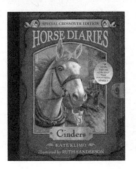

Cinders

KATE KLIMO
Illustrated by RUTH SANDERSON

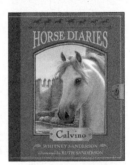

Calvino

WHITNEY SANDERSON
Illustrated by RUTH SANDERSON